HUMPHREY CARPENTER

Mr Majeika and the
School Caretaker

Illustrated by Frank Rodgers

Books by Humphrey Carpenter

MR MAJEIKA

MR MAJEIKA AND THE DINNER LADY

MR MAJEIKA AND THE GHOST TRAIN

MR MAJEIKA AND THE HAUNTED HOTEL

MR MAJEIKA AND THE LOST SPELL BOOK

MR MAJEIKA AND THE MUSIC TEACHER

MR MAJEIKA AND THE SCHOOL BOOK WEEK

MR MAJEIKA AND THE SCHOOL CARETAKER

MR MAJEIKA AND THE SCHOOL INSPECTOR

MR MAJEIKA AND THE SCHOOL PLAY

MR MAJEIKA AND THE SCHOOL TRIP

MR MAJEIKA ON THE INTERNET

MR MAJEIKA VANISHES

THE PUFFIN BOOK OF CLASSIC
CHILDREN'S STORIES (Ed.)

SHAKESPEARE WITHOUT THE BORING BITS
MORE SHAKESPEARE WITHOUT THE
BORING BITS

Contents

For Kate, who had the accident

PUFFIN BOOKS

Published by the Penguin Group
Penguin Books Ltd, 80 Strand, London WC2R 0RL, England
Penguin Group (USA) Inc., 375 Hudson Street, New York, New York 10014, USA
Penguin Group (Canada), 90 Eglinton Avenue East, Suite 700, Toronto, Ontario, Canada M4P 2Y3
(a division of Pearson Penguin Canada Inc.)
Penguin Ireland, 25 St Stephen's Green, Dublin 2, Ireland (a division of Penguin Books Ltd)
Penguin Group (Australia), 250 Camberwell Road, Camberwell,
Victoria 3124, Australia (a division of Pearson Australia Group Pty Ltd)
Penguin Books India Pvt Ltd, 11 Community Centre,
Panchsheel Park, New Delhi – 110 017, India
Penguin Group (NZ), cnr Airborne and Rosedale Roads, Albany,
Auckland 1310, New Zealand (a division of Pearson New Zealand Ltd)
Penguin Books (South Africa) (Pty) Ltd, 24 Sturdee Avenue,
Rosebank, Johannesburg 2196, South Africa

Penguin Books Ltd, Registered Offices: 80 Strand, London WC2R 0RL, England

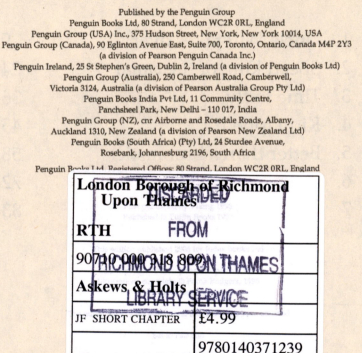

British Library Cataloguing in Publication Data
A CIP catalogue record for this book is available from the British Library

ISBN 0–140–37123–0

www.greenpenguin.co.uk

MIX
Paper from
responsible sources
FSC™ C018179

Penguin Books is committed to a sustainable future for our business, our readers and our planet. This book is made from Forest Stewardship Council™ certified paper.

1. *Uncle Wilf takes over*

It was three o'clock on a Friday afternoon, and everybody at St Barty's School was very, very sad. They were saying goodbye to Mr Jenks, who had been the school caretaker for as long as anyone could remember, but who was now retiring.

Mr Jenks was always kind and friendly. When you arrived at school in the morning, he always smiled and said "Good morning" to you, and called you by your name – though as he got older, he sometimes got the names wrong. This was because he had known hundreds and hundreds of children, all of whom had passed through the school since he first started working there. That had been a long time before Mr Potter became head teacher, and an even longer time before Mr Majeika had begun to teach Class Three.

Mr Majeika had been a wizard before he became a teacher, but Mr Jenks had always been a caretaker. Mr Majeika could do magic when he wanted to (though he wasn't supposed to now that he was a teacher), but Mr Jenks was always friendly, "and that," said Jody, "is just as nice as magic".

She and Thomas and Pete were sitting in the school hall, listening to Mr Potter making a speech about Mr Jenks, who was sitting on the platform next to him. Mr Potter finished the speech by handing a large parcel to Mr Jenks, and asking everyone to give him three cheers. "Hip, hip," said Mr Potter, and the whole school shouted "Hooray!" – except for a loud "Boo!" which came from behind Thomas, Pete, and Jody.

They turned round, though they knew perfectly well who was booing. "Hamish Bigmore!" said Jody angrily. "Why do you have to be so rude to Mr Jenks?" Hamish was the nastiest, rudest boy in Class Three.

"Silly old man," snorted Hamish. Jody knew why he was angry with Mr Jenks, who was the only person at St Barty's School who could make Hamish behave. Mr Jenks wasn't very big or very strong, but there was something about him which made Hamish stop being rude or

noisy whenever the caretaker looked at
him.

"Thank you, thank you," said Mr
Jenks, looking very happy, but also very
sad. He unwrapped his parcel. Inside
was a large cuckoo clock. Just at that
moment, it struck three, and the cuckoo
came out and cuckooed three times.
Everyone cheered. Hamish tried to boo
again, but Jody put her hand over his
mouth.

Mr Potter took Mr Jenks down to the hall door, and as everyone went out on their way home, Mr Jenks shook their hands. "Goodbye, Rosie," he said to Jody. "Goodbye, Fred," he said to Pete. "Goodbye, Timothy," he said to Thomas.

"Goodbye, Mr Jenks," they all said, not minding at all that he had got their names wrong.

Then it was Hamish Bigmore's turn. "Goodbye, Hamish," said Mr Jenks – nobody could ever mix Hamish up with someone else – "and do try not to be quite so naughty."

Hamish Bigmore scowled at Mr Jenks, and went past him without shaking his hand.

Outside, Jody, Thomas and Pete found Mr Majeika looking rather sad. "What's the matter, Mr Majeika?" they asked.

"I was just thinking," said Mr Majeika, "that people won't be as nice to me when I get old and have to retire. Mr Jenks has done so much to make St Barty's a nice place, and I've really done very little."

"That's nonsense, Mr Majeika," said Pete. "Your magic has made everything really fun for us." But he and Jody and Thomas gave each other a look, because the truth was, Mr Majeika hadn't done any magic for ages. Life in Class Three had been very ordinary, and very boring.

Just then, Mr Jenks came out of the hall, holding the cuckoo clock. He was looking very unhappy. "I can't believe it," he said miserably. "While I was shaking hands with everyone, someone managed to damage the clock. The cuckoo has been pulled out of its doorway and its spring is all bent. It

14

won't work properly."

"I can guess who that was," said
Thomas. "Can't you do something, Mr
Majeika?"

Mr Majeika scratched his head. "Well,
I oughtn't to," he said. "But we can't let
you go home with it like that, Mr Jenks."
He shut his eyes and waved his hands
and muttered some words, and the
cuckoo leaped to life. It whistled a jolly

tune, fluttered its wings, and then popped back through its door.

Mr Jenks was delighted. "Can't think how you did it, Mr Majeika," he said, beaming all over his face. "Just like magic!"

On Monday morning there was a notice by the school gate: CARETAKER WANTED. APPLY TO HEAD TEACHER. Mr Potter sat in his office, hoping that someone nice would knock on the door and ask for the job of caretaker. For a long while, nobody came. Then somebody did knock. "Come in," said Mr Potter hopefully.

The door opened. It was Hamish Bigmore. "Go away, Hamish!" said Mr Potter angrily. "I don't want to see you now. I'm holding job interviews. At least," he went on gloomily, "I would be, if anyone turned up for them."

"Well, they have now," snapped
Hamish. "Come on, Uncle!" He stepped
back, and a large, heavily built, very
tough-looking man stepped into Mr
Potter's office. He was so big he seemed
to fill the whole room.

"Er, how do you do?" said Mr Potter
nervously.

"Howjadoo?" answered the big man,

grasping Mr Potter's hand and pumping
it up and down so hard that Mr Potter
thought it was going to come off.

"Who are you?" gasped Mr Potter.

"This is my Uncle Wilf," said Hamish
from the doorway, laughing nastily.
"And you're going to give him the job of
school caretaker, Mr Potter, aren't you?"

"Yer, arncha?" said Uncle Wilf,
breathing nastily in Mr Potter's face and
grabbing hold of his hand again and
squeezing it very, very tight.

"Er, yes," gasped Mr Potter. "I
suppose I am."

Outside, several people had come to
apply for the job of school caretaker,
because they had seen it advertised in
the local newspaper. But Hamish had
written JOB FILLED, GO AWAY all over
Mr Potter's notice. So they went away.
And during school dinner, Mr Potter told

18

everyone that Hamish's Uncle Wilf was
going to be the new caretaker.

"We've got to do something about it,"
said Jody to Thomas and Pete during
dinner two weeks later. She didn't need
to say what she meant by "it". They both
knew she was talking about Hamish's
Uncle Wilf.

"I didn't know a caretaker could spoil
school for everyone like that," said

Thomas. "The other day, I was standing outside Mr Potter's office, writing my name on a list for a theatre visit while Hamish's Uncle Wilf was hoovering the carpet, and he came up to me and jabbed at my legs with the vacuum cleaner to get me out of the way. He nearly knocked me down!"

"You were lucky to be in the school building at all," said Pete. "The other day I was halfway home when I remembered I'd left my backpack in Class Three, with all my homework in it, so I ran back. But when I tried to get into school, Hamish's Uncle Wilf had locked all the doors. He shouted at me when I tried to get in and said he'd complain about me to Mr Potter if I didn't clear off."

"Talking about Mr Potter," said Jody, "he's really frightened of Hamish's Uncle

Wilf. The other day, Uncle Wilf arrived at school in a big black van. He drove it in through the gates and parked it in the middle of the playground, even though no one is supposed to drive in except the mobile library. But when Mr Potter asked him to move the van out into the road, Uncle Wilf shouted at him and waved a broom, and I thought he was going to hit Mr Potter. And Mr Potter just ran away."

"There's another thing about Uncle Wilf," Thomas whispered to Pete. "Things have been disappearing from people's bags and coat pockets and lunch boxes. I'm sure Uncle Wilf is stealing them, and giving them to Hamish – I thought I saw Hamish with a calculator that's gone missing from my bag."

"It's dreadful," said Mr Majeika, who had come up to them while they were talking. "I thought Hamish was as bad as people can get, but now I know there's worse."

"Can't you do something, Mr Majeika?" Jody asked.

Mr Majeika shook his head. "Mr Potter gave him the job," he said, "and it's not for me to interfere. But I've got some good news for you. Next Wednesday, we're all going to have a trip on a canal boat."

Class Three had been doing a project on rivers and canals, so everyone else was very pleased when they heard about the trip later on. Everyone except Hamish Bigmore. "What a rotten, stupid way to spend a day," he grumbled.

"We'll be starting from a boat-yard just down the road –" Mr Majeika said to the class, ignoring Hamish.

At that moment, the door burst open. It was Uncle Wilf, who had come in without knocking. "Gotta change a lightbulb," he shouted.

"Couldn't it wait until the next break?" asked Mr Majeika.

But Uncle Wilf paid no attention. He barged into the room, pushed people out of the way, climbed on to one of the tables, and took out a lightbulb which had been working perfectly well. Then he dropped it so that it burst, and broken glass went everywhere. By the time he had put in a new bulb and left the room, Mr Majeika was looking quite miserable.

"Oh dear," he said. "Well, it'll be nice to get away from him when we go to the canal – even if it's just for a day!"

2. *Speed king of the canal*

The day for the canal boat trip was fine
and sunny, and everyone was very
happy when they met at the canal boat-
yard not far from school – everyone
except Hamish Bigmore. "What's the
point of canals?" he grumbled. "Stupid,
smelly ditches. The only boat worth
going on is a mega-power-speedboat that
can go at a hundred miles an hour.
Zoom! Zoom! Zoom!" he shouted in the
ear of Melanie, who was always crying.
But today Melanie wasn't going to be
bullied by Hamish. She just stuck out her
tongue at him.

"We won't be going at a hundred
miles an hour on the canal boat,

Hamish," said Mr Majeika. He pointed at
a notice which said: SPEED LIMIT 4
MILES AN HOUR.

Hamish's eyes nearly popped out of
his head. "Four miles an hour?" he
screamed. "I can *walk* faster than that."

"Well, you're very welcome to walk if
you want to, Hamish," said Mr Majeika.
"You can walk along the path by the
canal and get the locks ready for us to go
through. But that's hard work, so I

expect you'd rather sit on the boat and
do nothing."

"You bet I would," grumbled Hamish.
"Wish I'd never come on this silly trip."

"But since you have, Hamish," said
Mr Majeika, "you must put on a life-
jacket like everyone else." He handed
Hamish a shiny yellow life-jacket, which
would keep him afloat if he fell into the
water.

"Life-jackets are for babies who can't
swim!" yelled Hamish. "I'm the best
swimmer in the school – I can do
hundreds of metres, and I'm training for
a cross-Channel race."

"That's rubbish, Hamish," said Jody.
"You know you always find some excuse
not to come to the swimming pool with
everyone else. I don't think you can
swim at all."

"Huh!" snorted Hamish angrily. "I'm

too good to swim with you lot, that's why I don't come." But Mr Majeika insisted that he put on a life-jacket with everyone else.

They all climbed on board, except Thomas and Pete, who had volunteered to walk ahead and get the locks ready. At first, the boat was steered by a man from the boat-yard, but when they reached the first lock, he got off. "I'll see you through this lock," he told them, while Thomas and Pete worked the gates and the

sluices which let water in and out. "After
that, you can manage by yourselves."

Mr Majeika looked a bit nervous when
the man said goodbye. Steering the boat
looked easy, but when he had tried it for
a few moments, with the man watching,
he had found it was actually quite hard.
You steered it with a long handle called
the tiller. It was all rather confusing. If
you pushed the tiller to the left, the boat
went to the right. If you pushed the tiller
to the right, the boat went to the left.
And if you made a mistake, there
weren't any brakes to stop the boat. The
only way to slow it down was to put the
engine into reverse.

"Oh dear," said Mr Majeika. "Doing
spells is much easier than making this
boat go in the right direction."

"Don't worry, Mr Majeika," said Jody,
when the man from the boat-yard had

gone. "We'll manage." She took over the tiller, and quickly got the hang of steering. The important thing was not to try to go too fast. If you did, the boat got out of control, and started to zigzag from one bank to another. Also, when you passed boats that were tied up along the bank, it was important to slow right down. Otherwise the water was stirred up so much that the other boats rocked up and down at their moorings and were

in danger of coming loose from the bank.

After half an hour, Thomas and Pete came on board, and Jody and Melanie got out and walked along the canalside path to get the next locks ready. This meant turning a handle to open a sluice – which was very heavy work – and then leaning heavily on the beam of the lock-gate to open it. It was very tiring, and Jody wasn't sorry when it was the turn of two other people.

By the time they stopped for lunch,

everyone had taken a turn at walking along the bank and working the locks – everyone except Hamish Bigmore. "I'm not doing that!" he shouted, when Mr Majeika told him it was his turn. "I came on this trip to ride on a boat, not to do slave labour. No way am I moving." And he lay on a bunk in the boat cabin, listening to loud pop music on his Walkman.

When lunch was finished, Mr Majeika said, "Now, Hamish, you really must take a turn at working the locks."

"Not till I've done some steering!" said Hamish. "Everyone else has had a turn at steering except me." This was true.

Mr Majeika sighed. "Very well," he said. "You can have five minutes at steering, but then you've got to do some real work." Hamish grinned and took the tiller.

To everyone's surprise, he steered the boat very well. He kept the engine running very slowly, so that the boat moved gently through the water, and when he came to narrow bridges he lined up the boat exactly right, so that it slipped through the small opening without bumping on either side. "Look, no bumps!" he shouted. "I'm much better than you lot." It was true that everyone else had bumped the boat a bit.

"His five minutes is up, Mr Majeika," said Thomas. "Do make him go and work the locks."

"I'll just give him a moment or two more," said Mr Majeika. "It's so nice to see Hamish doing something well."

It was just then that the trouble started. They were passing a sign on the bank which said: SLOW DOWN FOR MOORED BOATS. When Hamish saw it, he suddenly revved the engine up to full and, with a loud roaring noise, the boat began to move so fast that the moored boats bobbed wildly up and down. A very angry man stuck his head out of one of them. "Can't you read?" he shouted.

"Shut up, fathead," shouted Hamish. "I'm Hamish Bigmore, speed king of the canal!"

"Stop him, Mr Majeika," said Jody, who was standing with Mr Majeika in the front part of the boat, which is called the "bow". Mr Majeika tried to open the door which led into the cabin so that he could run through it and come out at the other end, the "stern", where Hamish was steering. But the door had banged shut and locked itself.

"I'll have to climb along the side of the boat," said Mr Majeika.

"Do be careful, Mr Majeika," shouted

Jody above the roaring noise of the engine. She was so worried that she followed him as he started to climb along the very narrow ledge which ran along the outside of the boat.

At that moment, they reached a bend in the canal. The boat took the bend at a frightening speed – and suddenly there was a very narrow bridge right in front of them. "Stop, Hamish!" yelled Mr Majeika. "Put the engine into reverse!"

Hamish threw the engine lever into reverse, but it was too late. The boat lurched forward and crashed into the bridge. Jody screamed – and so did Mr Majeika. The boat had squeezed their legs against the side of the bridge.

They clung on to the edge of the boat, as Hamish Bigmore at last brought the boat to a standstill and switched off the engine.

"Are you all right, Mr Majeika?" called Jody, whose legs were hurting badly.

"No," said Mr Majeika. "I don't think I am."

3. *Time to fly*

When they saw what had happened,
Thomas and Pete jumped on to the bank,
tied up the boat, and helped Jody and Mr
Majeika back on to the boat, where they
lay down. Their legs were cut and
bleeding and looked badly hurt.

"What are we going to do?" said

Thomas, looking very worried. "We're miles from any houses."

"Mr Majeika, can't you do some magic?" said Pete. "Surely you know a spell to make you and Jody better?"

"I wish I did," groaned Mr Majeika. "There *is* a spell for that in my spell book. But I haven't got the book here and I can't remember it."

"Perhaps the best thing would be to start the boat again," said Thomas, "then we'll take it on to where there are houses, and then we can phone for an ambulance."

"Please be quick," said Jody. "I think our legs are broken – at least I'm sure mine are – and we need to get to hospital as soon as possible."

"I've been looking at the map," said Pete, sounding worried, "and there aren't any houses for ages. What on earth are we going to do?"

Melanie, who usually started crying as soon as anything went wrong, had been completely silent. Suddenly she said, "What about your magic carpet, Mr Majeika?" She had remembered Mr Majeika's first day at St Barty's School, when he had arrived on a magic carpet.

"That would have helped, Melanie," said Mr Majeika. "But I haven't got it here."

"No, but you once magicked another carpet into flying," said Melanie. "Couldn't you do that again?"

"I suppose I could," said Mr Majeika, shutting his eyes because his legs were hurting so much. "But there isn't a carpet in the boat cabin, is there?"

"What I meant, Mr Majeika," said Melanie, "is that you could magic *the boat* into flying. Then you and Jody could get to hospital very quickly."

"That's brilliant," said Thomas. "But can you do it, Mr Majeika?"

Five minutes later, two old men fishing by the side of the canal were having an argument about the size of a fish one of them had caught.

"It was sixty centimetres long," said the one who had caught it.

"No it wasn't," said the other. "It was only about twenty centimetres. You're always telling whopping great stories which aren't true."

"And I've had enough of your rudeness," said the first old man, getting to his feet and marching off, over a stile and across a field.

The second old man started to pack up his fishing rod. Suddenly there was a noise overhead, like a low-flying aircraft.

He looked up – and nearly fell into the canal with surprise.

A moment later, he was running across the field after the first old man. "Jim!" he called. "Jim! You'll never guess what I've seen – a boat that flies!"

The first old man turned round and laughed at him. "Now who's telling whopping great stories which aren't true?" he mocked.

At the Accident and Emergency entrance of the Bartyshire County Hospital, two ambulancemen were folding up a stretcher and putting it back into their ambulance, when there was a loud whooshing noise, and something very big came down from the sky and landed next to them.

The men stared. "Bert, what did you put in that coffee I was just drinking?"

said one of them. "I'm seeing things. I'm seeing a canal boat that flies."

"So am I, Fred," said the other, "so am I."

Pete, who had been steering the boat as it flew from the canal to the hospital (he found that he could use the tiller to steer it), climbed off and went up to the ambulancemen. "Can you help us, please?" he said. "We have two injured passengers on board. We think they've got broken legs."

The ambulancemen looked very white in the face. "We're not feeling too good ourselves," said the one called Fred. "You've just given us a bit of a shock. But we'll get two stretchers on to the boat and get the patients off right away."

In a few moments, Mr Majeika and Jody had been carefully lifted off the boat and taken into the Accident and Emergency department, where a kind nurse and doctor attended to them at once. The cuts on their legs were cleaned up and they were taken through to the X-ray department, so that pictures could be taken to find out if their legs were broken.

"I'm afraid they *are* broken," said the doctor a few minutes later. "But don't worry. We'll soon have them mended."

"Will I have plaster on my legs?" said Jody. She hoped she would, because then all her friends could write their names on it.

"Oh yes," said the doctor. "You'll be in plaster for weeks and weeks."

"Hooray!" said Jody. "Won't that be fun, Mr Majeika?"

"I suppose so," said Mr Majeika gloomily. He didn't think it would be fun at all.

Meanwhile the rest of Class Three were ringing up their parents from the payphone at the hospital entrance, to say what had happened and arrange to be collected. All except Hamish Bigmore. He had found another payphone, in a different part of the building, and he was making a secret call.

"Is that Uncle Wilf?" he said, giggling nastily. "This is your nephew, Hamish.

43

If you and You Know Who come quickly
to the Bartyshire Hospital, you'll get the
chance you've been waiting for!''

4. *Kidnapped!*

At five o'clock that afternoon, Jody opened her eyes. She was lying in a comfortable bed but, though her legs had stopped hurting, they were feeling strange. She lifted her head off the pillow and looked down at them. Both of them were in plaster.

"Can I be the first to write my name on them?" said a voice. It was Thomas. He was sitting by her bedside, and in the dim light of the hospital ward Jody hadn't seen him.

"No, I want to be the first," said another voice. It was Pete. He was sitting on the other side of the bed.

"There's no need to quarrel," said Jody. "One of you can write on my left leg, the other on my right leg." So they did.

A nurse came up to Jody's bed, took her temperature, felt her pulse, and made some notes on a chart. "How are you feeling?" she asked.

"Not bad, thank you," said Jody. "When can I get up?"

"We can fetch you a wheelchair now, if you like," said the nurse. "You'll need to get used to going around in it. Then in a few weeks we can take off this heavy plaster, and put something more lightweight on your legs to protect them, and then you can start going around on crutches. Your legs weren't badly broken – the bones are just cracked a bit – so they won't take long to mend."

"Could I really get into the wheelchair now?" asked Jody. The nurse smiled, and went off to fetch it. "How's Mr Majeika getting on?" Jody asked Thomas and Pete.

"We don't know," said Pete. "We haven't been to see him yet. He's in another ward."

"Maybe we could all go when you've got your wheelchair," said Thomas.

The nurse came back with the wheelchair. She and another nurse helped Jody out of bed and into it. Thomas and Pete wanted to push the chair, but the nurse said that Jody must learn to work it herself. It wasn't very

hard – you just turned the wheels with
your hands.

"Can I go round the hospital with my
friends?" Jody asked.

The two nurses looked at each other.
"Well, we shouldn't really let you," said
the first nurse. "But if you promise to be
back in ten minutes, I expect it won't do
any harm."

They opened the door of the ward, so
Jody could get her chair through it, and
then they set off down the passage,
which was very long. All kinds of notices
pointed in different directions: X-RAY,
PHYSIOTHERAPY, SURGICAL WARD,
MATERNITY WARD, GERIATRIC
WARD, ACCIDENT & EMERGENCY.
"Which way shall we go?" said Pete.

"If we start with Accident and
Emergency," said Jody, "they should be
able to tell us which ward he's in."

48

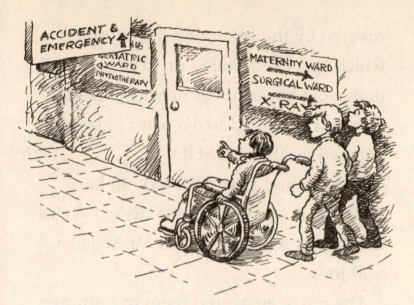

"It won't be the Maternity Ward," said Pete. "That's where people go to have babies."

"And it won't be the Geriatric Ward," said Thomas, "because 'geriatric' means old people, and Mr Majeika isn't old."

They reached Accident and Emergency. There was no one there except a nurse sitting behind a desk. Her cap was very large, and hid the top half of her face. The bottom half was mostly covered by the collar of her uniform, which had been pulled up very high. All that could be seen was her nose, which was very long and had a pair of glasses perched on the end of it.

Thomas and Pete, and Jody in her wheelchair, went up to the desk. "We're looking for someone called Mr Majeika," said Jody.

The nurse answered them in a strange squeaky voice, "Nobody here with that name. Push off!"

Jody, Thomas and Pete looked at each other. It wasn't the way that nurses usually behave, and her appearance was very, very odd.

"He was brought in this afternoon with broken legs," said Thomas. "We need to know where they've taken him."

"None of your business!" squeaked the nurse. "Now, push off, or *you'll* get something broken."

"Listen," said Pete angrily, "he must be in one of the wards. Just tell us which one, please."

The nurse pointed with a finger. "That one over there!" she snapped.

They all looked in the direction she was pointing in. A notice said MATERNITY WARD.

"He can't be in there," said Jody. "Do tell us, please."

"All right, dearies, I'll tell you," said

the nurse, getting up from her desk.
"Come along with Nurse Ermintrude
and see where stupid old – I mean, nice,
clever – Mr Majeika has been put, tee
hee!" She came out from behind the
desk, and they could see that she was
wearing big boots beneath her uniform.

"I don't think we should go with her,"
whispered Jody.

"But we've got to find Mr Majeika,"
whispered Thomas. "Something funny is
going on, and he may need rescuing."

"Come along, dearies!" squeaked
Nurse Ermintrude. They followed her
through several swing doors and down a
dark, narrow passage. Suddenly Nurse
Ermintrude stopped and opened a door.
"He's in there!" she squeaked. "In you
all go!"

Thomas and Pete did as they were
told, but Jody lingered in the passage.

"Be careful," she whispered to them.

Nurse Ermintrude turned to her.
"Come along, dearie," she cooed. "Don't
you want to see your friend, Mr Majeika?
Well, come in here, dearie, and you will
– for the last time!" And she grabbed the
handles of Jody's wheelchair and pushed
it through the doorway.

"This is just a cupboard full of mops

and brooms," said Thomas. "There's no one in here." But it was too late. The door had been slammed and locked. They were shut in!

"Tee hee," came Nurse Ermintrude's voice, and they heard her boots thumping away down the passage. "Got you this time, my dearies. And now to get Majeika!"

They all looked at each other, and said, "Wilhelmina Worlock!"

Wilhelmina Worlock was a witch. She was the enemy of Mr Majeika and Class Three – except for Hamish Bigmore, who was always helping her with her mischief. She called him her Star Pupil.

"What are we going to do now?" said Thomas miserably, rattling the handle of the cupboard door. "I suppose if we shout "Help!" for long enough, someone will come."

"But by that time, she'll have done some harm to Mr Majeika," said Pete. "We've got to escape as quickly as we can."

Jody was looking around her – and upwards too. "Look," she said. "There's a kind of window in the roof. Maybe if you could get up there, you could open it and climb out."

"Stand underneath it," Pete said to Thomas, "and I'll climb on your shoulders."

"No, *you* stand there," Thomas said to Pete, "and *I'll* climb up."

"Oh, do stop arguing," said Jody. "There's no time to lose."

Pete climbed on Thomas's shoulders. "Yes, the window opens," he said. "And gosh! Guess what I can see!"

"I don't want to hear about the view," said Thomas. "Just get that window

open and get out of it before my
shoulders get broken too. We've got to
rescue Mr Majeika!"

"But that's the point!" shouted Pete. "I
can see him – I can see Mr Majeika! He's
on a stretcher, and a nurse and a doctor
are putting him into an ambulance. And
there's someone helping them. How
odd. It's Hamish Bigmore . . . Oh no!"

"What is it?" said Jody anxiously.

"It's not an ambulance, it's a big black van. And it's not a doctor and a nurse, it's Wilhelmina Worlock and Uncle Wilf. Mr Majeika is being kidnapped!"

5. *Better than a broomstick*

Before Jody and Thomas had time to say a word, Pete had scrambled out of the window and vanished. "Come back!" shouted Thomas. "What about us?"

"Perhaps he'll run round and unlock the door," said Jody.

"I bet he doesn't," said Thomas. "My brother never thinks."

"Listen!" said Thomas. "I can hear Pete shouting something." They listened, and could certainly hear Pete's voice. But they couldn't make out what he was saying. And then there was the sound of Uncle Wilf's van being started.

"Oh no," said Jody. "I think they're driving off. It doesn't sound as if Pete has managed to rescue Mr Majeika."

They could still hear Pete shouting, and now there was a loud noise of someone banging on what sounded like the side of the van. But then the van drove off, and the banging noise faded away with it.

There was silence. "What did I tell you?" said Thomas. "Just like my brother to go off on his own adventure, leaving us stuck here. It isn't fair."

"I don't know that he's having an adventure," said Jody. "Perhaps

Wilhelmina Worlock and Uncle Wilf have kidnapped him too."

"I almost wish they have," said Thomas. "It would serve him right for being so silly. Oh, if only we could get out of here." He rattled the door but it remained firmly locked, and there was no sound of anyone in the passage outside. "Help!" Thomas shouted, but no one was near enough to hear.

"Thomas," said Jody after a few moments, "I've been thinking and I've got an idea. Do you remember that Mr Majeika made the canal boat fly?"

"Of course I remember," said Thomas. "It's about the only exciting thing that's happened for years and years and years. Well, several weeks," he added, because it hadn't been *that* long since Mr Majeika last did some magic.

"And do you remember how he did

it?" asked Jody eagerly.

"Of course I remember," said Thomas.

"That's wonderful!' gasped Jody. "I was hoping that you might remember, but I didn't think you would. How *did* he do it?"

"He did it by magic, of course," said Thomas.

"I know that, you fathead!" said Jody crossly. "I meant, do you remember which spell he used? The actual words?"

Thomas shook his head. "No, I don't," he said. "He was just whispering them to himself, lying on a bunk on the boat."

"That's right," said Jody. "He was whispering because his legs were hurting so much that he didn't really want to talk. I was lying next to him, and I *think* I can remember some of them . . ." She shut her eyes, and started to whisper some strange words.

"That sounds like the right sort of thing," said Thomas.

"I wish I could remember the rest of them," said Jody, opening her eyes. "But I don't think I – Oops! Help! *Look*!"

Thomas didn't need to be told to look. His eyes were almost popping out of his head.

Jody's wheelchair was rising up. Just a few inches at first, then slowly up and up and up. The wheels were hovering in front of Thomas's eyes. Then – whoosh! The chair lifted very fast, just like a rocket taking off, and whizzed right through the open window above them, which luckily was big enough for the chair to go through it.

"Help!" shouted Jody. "I'm flying!" without thinking what she was doing, she grabbed hold of the wheelchair brake

and pulled it tightly. It worked! The chair stopped in mid-air, hovering over the open window.

"Let's see if I can make it move again," she said. She took off the brake, and the chair began to move upwards. "I'll try the wheels," she called. She turned one of the wheels a little, and the chair moved to the left. She turned the other, and it moved to the right. Then she turned them both, and it went down, nearly dropping through the window again. "This is wonderful!" she called. "I can go and rescue Mr Majeika."

"You might think about rescuing me too," said Thomas. "I don't terribly want to spend the rest of my life in this broom cupboard."

"What did you say?" called Jody, because it was difficult to hear Thomas from up in the air.

"I said *broom cupboard*," shouted Thomas.

"That's it!" yelled Jody excitedly. "I've got it! If the spell works for a boat and a wheelchair, it might work for a –" The wind carried her last word away, and Thomas didn't hear it.

"Did you say a *room*?" he shouted. "I've never heard of a flying room."

"Not a *room*, you idiot," Jody shouted back. "A *broom*! If witches fly on brooms, so can you. Grab one of them quickly, and say the words."

The cupboard was full of brooms and brushes and mops, but Thomas couldn't imagine how he could fly safely on any of them. Then he saw something stacked up behind them. "I've got it!" he shouted. He dived in among all the things, and pulled out a big vacuum cleaner. It was shaped like a sausage on wheels. "This'll be safe to sit on," he called. "But I can't remember the magic words."

Jody steered the wheelchair down a few feet, so that it was hovering in the opening of the window. Then she called out the magic words.

"It's working!" cried Thomas. The vacuum cleaner had taken off from the floor of the broom cupboard. He was sitting astride it, holding on as tight as he could. "Here I come!" he shouted, pulling the nose of the vacuum cleaner upwards.

"Careful!" called Jody. "Let me get out of the way first." She steered the wheelchair up again, just as Thomas zoomed out of the window at high speed. He circled round and round the chair, shouting "Look at me! I'm flying!"

"You should have taken off the pipe thing," shouted Jody. From the front of

the vaccum cleaner hung a long pipe
with a nozzle at the end – except that it
wasn't hanging any more. It was waving
around wildly like the trunk of a mad
elephant.

"Never mind," called Thomas.
"There's no time to waste. We're off to
rescue Mr Majeika!"

Meanwhile, about two miles away, Uncle
Wilf was driving his big black van very
fast along a narrow country lane. Beside
him in the passenger seat, Wilhelmina
Worlock was rubbing her hands with
glee. "Tee hee!" she was saying. "No
escape for you this time, Majeika!"

In the back of the van, Mr Majeika was
lying on a stretcher. Both his legs were in
plaster, but Wilhelmina and Uncle Wilf
weren't taking any chances. They'd tied
his hands behind his back and fixed a

large gag over his mouth, so that he couldn't say any spells. In fact he didn't look as if he'd ever say anything again. His eyes were shut, and he only moved when the van swerved, which made him roll around the floor.

Next to him, on a pile of old sacks, sat Hamish Bigmore, stuffing his mouth from a very large box of chocolates.

"Hasn't your Star Pupil done well?" he called out to Wilhelmina, splattering Mr Majeika with bits of chocolate when he opened his mouth.

"Yes, dearie," said Wilhelmina. "But don't eat yourself sick. Wilhelmina has got another job for her Star Pupil right away."

"Whassat?" grumbled Hamish, who didn't want to do any jobs.

"Wilhelmina wants her Star Pupil to go back to that silly old school of his," cooed Miss Worlock, "and give them a ransom note."

"A what?" spluttered Hamish.

"A letter telling them to give Wilhelmina five million pounds, otherwise something very, very nasty will happen to our friend Majeika. That's right, isn't it?" she cooed, turning to Uncle Wilf.

"Yer," said Uncle Wilf, "somethink very narrsty." And he and Wilhelmina both laughed horribly.

Just at that moment, there was a sudden banging and crashing above their heads. "A thunderstorm," growled Uncle Wilf, looking nervous. "I'm frightened of thunderstorms." He started to shiver.

Wilhelmina rolled down the window on her side and looked out. "It's not a thunderstorm," she snapped. "It's some stupid kid on the roof of the van. One of Majeika's little friends. We'll have to shake him off."

"And look!" shouted Hamish, peering through the back window of the van. "There are two strange creatures flying after us. Help! We're being pursued!"

"Tee hee," cackled Wilhelmina. "We know what to do about that, don't we, Wilf?"

"Yer," growled Uncle Wilf. "We're gonna do somethink very, *very* narrsty. Har har har!"

6. *How to find five million*

At a quarter to nine the next morning, Mr Potter came into Class Three and told them: "I'm going to have to teach you today, because Mr Majeika is still in hospital after his accident."

"Is Jody still in hospital too?" asked Melanie. "She hasn't turned up this morning."

"And Thomas and Pete aren't here either," said Pandora Green.

"Hamish Bigmore's not here," said someone else.

"Oh dear," said Mr Potter. "So many people are missing. I can't take the register because it's locked up in my office, and our school caretaker hasn't turned up this morning either, and he has the key."

"My mum was driving me back from a friend's house in the country quite late last night," said Melanie, "and the caretaker's big black van overtook us. It was going so fast it nearly pushed us into the ditch."

"Never mind that now," said Mr Potter. "We'd better get on with a lesson."

At that moment, the door of Class Three began to open very slowly. When the gap was just wide enough, an envelope was pushed through it by a hand. On the envelope was written, in big black writing, the words RANSOM DEMAND.

"Look, Mr Potter!" called everyone.

Mr Potter took the envelope from the hand and opened the door fully. But the

owner of the hand had run away.

"I'm sure it was Hamish Bigmore,"
said Melanie. "I heard him laughing as
he ran off."

Mr Potter was about to open the
envelope, when there was a strange
whooshing noise outside in the
playground. Everyone ran to look out of
the window. "It's Jody in a flying
wheelchair!" shouted Pandora.

"And Thomas on what looks like a

flying elephant," said Pandora. "Oh no, it's a Hoover! It must be some of Mr Majeika's magic, but there's no sign of Mr Majeika."

Thomas climbed off the vacuum cleaner and helped Jody get her wheelchair through the door into the school building. "You're late," Mr Potter said to them both, when they finally arrived in Class Three. "And Thomas, I don't know where you got that vacuum cleaner, but you must take it back, as soon as school is finished this afternoon." So much magic had been done at St Barty's School since Mr Majeika arrived that Mr Potter had stopped being surprised at anything unusual.

"There's no time to lose, Mr Potter," gasped Jody. "We need your help to rescue Mr Majeika!"

"Rescue him?" repeated Mr Potter, scratching his head. "I thought he was in hospital."

"Miss Worlock and Hamish's Uncle Wilf have stolen him from the hospital," said Thomas, holding on to a table to steady himself because he was feeling very airsick after his long flight on the vacuum cleaner.

"We've been chasing them all night," said Jody. "When they saw we were after

76

them, they played a dirty trick. They
drove the van to a power station with
huge cooling towers, so that we flew
straight into the towers and nearly had a
bad accident. By the time we'd got
ourselves sorted out again, they'd
vanished."

"It took us ages to find them," said
Thomas. "But in the end we saw where
they are."

"They've taken Mr Majeika to an
enormous quarry, a huge hole in the
ground, with water and rocks at the
bottom. And they're going to push him
over the edge if –"

"If we don't give them lots and lots of
money," said Thomas, interrupting Jody.

Mr Potter scratched his head again.
"I'll certainly do what I can to help," he
said. "I've got about thirty-six pounds in
the dinner-money box, but it's locked up

in my office. We'll have to ask Hamish's Uncle Wilf for the key."

"That's not nearly enough, Mr Potter," said Jody. "Open the letter."

Mr Potter tore open the envelope, and read:

Dear Potty Potter

You must bring FIVE MILLION POUNDS to the Old Quarry by twelve o'clock, or Majeika will MEET HIS END, tee hee hee!

From your Old Chum

   Wilhelmina

PS Also, if you don't bring the money, I'LL TURN YOU ALL INTO TOADS!

Melanie began to cry. "It's all right," said Thomas. "We'll make sure no one turns you into a toad, Melanie."

"It's not that," sobbed Melanie. "I'm frightened for Mr Majeika. They can have all the money that I've got in the post office, but there's only about thirty pounds."

Everyone else offered money, and Mr Potter wrote down how much it would come to if they all handed over their savings. "I've got two thousand pounds in the post office myself," he said, "and we can give them that too." But even with his kind offer, the total only came to £2,836.27.

"What on earth are we going to do?" said Thomas, desperately.

Jody was looking round the room. "I've got an idea. Has anybody seen the Monopoly set?"

An hour later, the school minibus, with Mr Potter driving and Class Three

crammed into the back, turned off the
main road and followed a sign saying TO
OLD QUARRY. "Slow down, Mr
Potter," said Jody, "otherwise we'll fall
straight over the edge."

"Park by that tree over there," said
Thomas. "The one they've tied my
brother to."

"They've tied your brother to a tree?"
said Mr Potter. "Goodness, you never
mentioned that."

"Oh, Pete will be all right," said Thomas. "It's Mr Majeika I want to rescue. Well, I don't mind if Pete gets rescued too, I suppose."

"Pete was very brave," said Jody. "They drove the van very, very fast so as to make him fall off the roof. But he held on tight, and when they stopped, he tried to fight them, so they tied him up."

"Here we are," said Jody. "Stop the van here, Mr Potter."

No sooner had Mr Potter put on the brakes than a hand was tapping at the window of the driver's door. It was Wilhelmina Worlock. "Hello, dearie," she said to Mr Potter. "You're all nice and early. And have you got lots of lovely cash for little Wilhelmina?"

"Here you are," said Mr Potter, handing over a parcel. "There are exactly five million pounds in there. And you'll also find that we have given you the ownership of lots of streets and hotels and famous buildings in London."

"That's very nice of you, dearie," said Miss Worlock. "Poor old Wilhelmina doesn't usually get treated so kindly. In that case, you can have your friend Majeika back right away."

Everything might have gone all right if Pete, who was tied to the tree, hadn't started laughing. He had seen what was inside the envelope when Miss Worlock opened it and started to count the banknotes. "What's up with you, you little weasel?" she snarled, turning on him.

"Here, let me look," squeaked another voice. It was Hamish Bigmore. He ran up and snatched some of the banknotes from Wilhelmina.

"Give them back, Hamish Bigmouth!"

she shrieked at him. "Who said you could have any?"

"You're welcome to it," laughed Hamish. "It isn't real money at all. It's from a game called Monopoly, and it isn't worth a penny."

"Is that so, dearie?" said Miss Worlock in a very nasty voice. She turned, and called over to where Uncle Wilf's big black van was parked on the edge of the quarry. "Let it go!" she shrieked.

The van began to roll forward. The driver's door opened, and Uncle Wilf jumped out. "Good riddance to all stoopid wizards!" he shouted, giving the van an extra push as it rolled past him, over the edge of the quarry.

7. *Hamish in the swim*

Everyone gasped in horror – and then
cheered – because the van, after starting
to fall down into the quarry, had
suddenly risen up in the air. "It's flying!"
said Thomas to Jody.

"I know it is," said Jody. "Ssh! I need
to concentrate."

Wilhelmina and Uncle Wilf looked at

each other in horror. Then they began to run. The van had turned round and was coming straight at them. They ran and ran – they ran right over the edge of the quarry.

But they didn't fall. They turned into huge black geese, flapped their wings, and flew away till they were out of sight. Everyone cheered again as the van came to rest on the ground at the edge of the quarry. Then the back door opened, and out stepped Mr Majeika. His legs weren't in plaster. He was perfectly all right again.

"You're cured, Mr Majeika!" said Thomas. "That's wonderful. Did you remember the spell?"

"Yes," said Mr Majeika. "I did. When I realized the van was flying, and that I wasn't going to crash down into the bottom of the quarry, I was so happy that the words of the spell to mend my legs came back to me."

"Do you mean it wasn't you, Mr Majeika, who made the van fly?" asked Melanie.

"No, Melanie," answered Mr Majeika. "When I was kidnapped by Wilhelmina and that wicked brother of hers – yes, he was really her brother, Wilfred Worlock, a very wicked wizard, and not Hamish's uncle at all – they cast a spell to stop me doing my own spells. But when someone else made the van fly by magic, that broke their spell. I wonder who it was?"

Thomas turned to Jody. "It was you, Jody, wasn't it?" he said.

Jody nodded. "I suddenly thought that I could do it," she said. "And it worked!"

"Well, Jody, you've saved my life." said Mr Majeika. "So the least I can do in return is to mend your legs." He

muttered a spell, the plaster dropped off
Jody's legs and she jumped to her feet.
"Hooray!" she shouted.

"But where's Hamish?" said Thomas.

They all looked around. "There he is!"
shouted Pandora. "He's running off
down that lane, past the sign which says
TO THE CANAL."

"Get him, Jody," said Thomas. "Like
you got Miss Worlock and Uncle Wilf."

Jody shut her eyes and muttered the

spell which had made the van fly. It rose up in the air and began to chase Hamish Bigmore down the lane. Everyone heard a splash.

When they got to the canal, Hamish was floundering about in it, waving his arms and legs wildly. "Help!" he shouted. "I can't swim!"

"Told you so," said Jody.

"I think it's time he had lessons," said Pete, who had been untied from his tree. "Don't you, Mr Majeika?"

"Yes," said Mr Majeika. "And I know who can teach him. We'll be needing another school caretaker now, so let's ask Mr Jenks to stop being retired and come back to St Barty's. And when he's not caretaking, he can give Hamish swimming lessons. Would you like blue waterwings, Hamish? Or do you prefer pink?"

Hamish opened his mouth to make a
rude reply, but all that came out was a
great deal of canal water.

Mr Majeika
and the
Haunted Hotel

Humphrey Carpenter

Spooks and spectres at the *Green Banana*!

Class Three of St Barty's are off on an outing to
Hadrian's Wall with their teacher, Mr Majeika (who
happens to be a magician). Stranded in the fog when the
tyres of their coach are mysteriously punctured, they
take refuge in a nearby hotel called the Green Banana.
Soon some very spooky things start to happen. Strange
lights, ghostly sounds and vanishing people . . .

Mr Majeika

and the
School Book Week

Humphrey Carpenter

"Gosh," said Thomas, "isn't that Robin Hood?"

When St Barty's School have their Book Week, you can
be sure that Mr Majeika brings the characters alive – but
how can he make them go back into their books? And
when a new PE teacher organizes an Olympic Sports
Day and has Hamish Bigmore winning every event –
there has to be magic in the air! This is not going to be
an ordinary week . . .

Also in Young Puffin

Mr Majeika

and the
Music Teacher

Humphrey Carpenter

"Music teacher? What music teacher? I don't know anything about any music teacher."

It's a new term at St Barty's and the school is in uproar. Awful noises come from Class Three, angry parents fill the school and poor Mr Majeika is really frightened. Why? A new music teacher is coming who plans to start a school orchestra, and as only Mr Majeika knows, Wilhelmina Worlock is a witch!

Also in Young Puffin

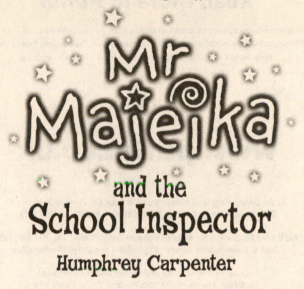

Mr Majeika

and the
School Inspector

Humphrey Carpenter

"Use of magic by teacher strictly forbidden."

Poor Mr Majeika gains so many penalty points when
the nasty Mr Postlethwaite, a school inspector, comes to
inspect St Barty's School that he very nearly loses his
teacher's licence. However, at Barty Castle Mr Majeika
gets his revenge when he arranges for the inspector to
have a very chilling encounter!

Read more in Puffin

For complete information about books available from Puffin – and Penguin – and how to order them, contact us at the appropriate address below. Please note that for copyright reasons the selection of books varies from country to country.

www.puffin.co.uk

In the United Kingdom: Please write to Dept EP, Penguin Books Ltd,
Bath Road, Harmondsworth, West Drayton, Middlesex UB7 0DA

In the United States: Please write to Penguin Group (USA), Inc., P.O. Box 12289,
Dept B, Newark, New Jersey 07101–5289 or call 1–800–788–6262

In Canada: Please write to Penguin Books Canada Ltd,
10 Alcorn Avenue, Suite 300, Toronto, Ontario M4V 3B2

In Australia: Please write to Penguin Books Australia Ltd,
250 Camberwell Road, Camberwell, Victoria 3124

In New Zealand: Please write to Penguin Books (NZ) Ltd,
Private Bag 102902, North Shore Mail Centre, Auckland 10

In India: Please write to Penguin Books India Pvt Ltd,
11 Panscheel Shopping Centre, Panscheel Park, New Delhi 110 017

In the Netherlands: Please write to Penguin Books Netherlands bv,
Postbus 3507, NL–1001 AH Amsterdam

In Germany: Please write to Penguin Books Deutschland GmbH,
Metzlerstrasse 26, 60594 Frankfurt am Main

In Spain: Please write to Penguin Books S. A., Bravo Murillo 19,
1° B, 28015 Madrid

In Italy: Please write to Penguin Italia s.r.l.,
Via Felice Casati 20, I–20124 Milano

In France: Please write to Penguin France S. A.,
17 rue Lejeune, F–31000 Toulouse

In Japan: Please write to Penguin Books Japan, Ishikiribashi Building,
2–5–4, Suido, Bunkyo-ku, Tokyo 112

In South Africa: Please write to Longman Penguin Southern Africa (Pty) Ltd,
Private Bag X08, Bertsham 2013